W9-BXP-623

FESTIVAL
READERS

Maurice Sendak's Little Bear: Father Bear's Special Day

Based on the animated television series *Little Bear* produced by Nelvana.

Based on the series of books written by Else Holmelund Minarik and illustrated by Maurice Sendak

Printed in the U.S.A.
Library of Congress catalog card number: 2002107440
www.harperchildrens.com

3 4 5 6 7 8 9 10

First Edition

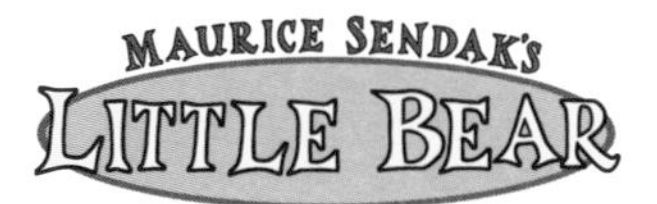

BY ELSE HOLMELUND MINARIK
ILLUSTRATIONS BY TERI LEE

"Happy Father's Day!" said
Little Bear, as he bounced on
Mother and Father's bed.
"Are you ready? Are you ready?"
asked Little Bear.

“I think your father is ready to sleep just a little bit longer,” said Mother Bear. “Why don’t we see about breakfast?”

Little Bear asked, “What shall I give
Father Bear as a present?”
“I think the best present of all
is just being your own sweet self,”
said Mother Bear.

At breakfast, Father Bear asked
Little Bear if he would like
to go fishing.

"Oh, yes!" said Little Bear.

"I can bait the hooks!"

"Very good," said Father Bear.

"Now pack up the fishing box

and we can be off!"

And so they set off to go fishing.

Little Bear said, "I want to be your helper all day long."

"What a nice present," said Father Bear.

As they walked, they met Emily.

She was carrying a fishing rod.

“Good morning,” she said.

“Are you going fishing, too?”

Little Bear wished Emily would fish somewhere else.

After all, it was father’s special day.

They walked a bit farther,

and there was Duck.

"Are you going fishing?" asked Duck.

"Yes, we are," said Father Bear.

"Would you like to join us?"

"Oh, yes!" Duck replied.

And so Duck joined Father Bear,
Little Bear, and Emily.

They couldn't quite fit on the path.

Little Bear ended up walking

beside Duck.

Up ahead, Emily and Father Bear

talked about fishing.

Little Bear felt left out.

Duck wanted to chat. "I hope you

brought plenty of worms," she said.

"Fish love nice, juicy worms."

Little Bear looked in his fishing box.

He had forgotten the worms!

“I forgot to pack worms!” said Little Bear.

“Don’t worry, Little Bear,” said Duck.

“I can catch some worms for you.”

By now they were almost at the lake.
The air was crisp and the sun was
shining and the flowers were blooming.
It was a lovely day!

At the lake, Father Bear took off
his jacket and sat down on a rock.

Emily set her fishing rod down

and tied a hook onto her line.

“Little Bear, please bring me
the fishing box,” said Father Bear.
Father Bear looked inside.
“I see we have hooks, and we have
lines, but I don’t see any worms,”
said Father Bear.

"Don't worry," said Duck.

"I can dig up some worms!

I'll get some lively ones!"

And she did.

In a few minutes, Duck gave

Father Bear a wriggling,

wiggling bunch of worms to

use for bait.

"I caught a fish!" shouted Emily,
as she pulled in her line.
"That's a big one!" said Father Bear.
"You should be proud of yourself."

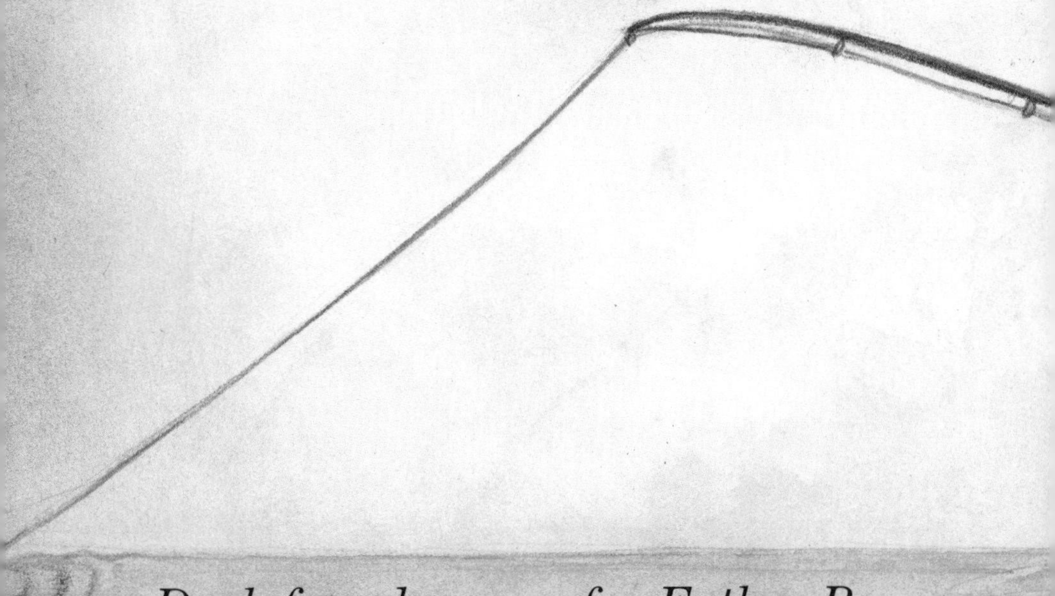

Duck found worms for Father Bear,
and now Emily has caught a fish,
thought Little Bear.
What have I done for Father Bear?

“Little Bear, would you bait my hook?”
asked Father Bear.
“Oh, yes!” said Little Bear.
Duck’s worms were awfully wiggly.
They were getting away from Little Bear.

“Let me help you, Little Bear,” said Emily.
“It takes practice.”
She put the worm on the hook
and gave the rod to Father Bear.

Little Bear felt very sad.

He had forgotten the worms,

and Duck had found some.

He couldn't bait the hook,

and Emily had done it for him.

After an hour, Emily went home.

Duck fell asleep in the warm sun.

Little Bear said to Father Bear,
"I'm sorry I wasn't very helpful.
I was going to be your helper all day,
and I guess I didn't do such a good job."

Father Bear looked at Little Bear
and said, "You are a wonderful bear,
and having you for a son is the
only Father's Day present I want."
He gave Little Bear a big kiss.

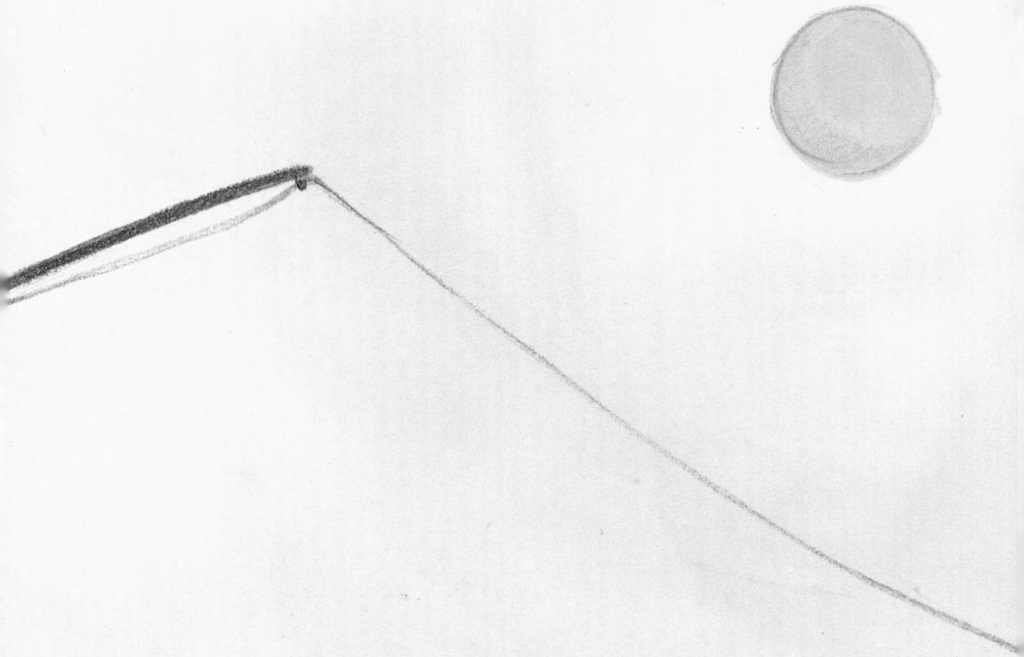

"Happy Father's Day, Father Bear!"
said Little Bear.
"Thank you, Little Bear," said Father Bear.
"And now we should go home for lunch."

Duck was sleeping so nicely that they left her napping in the sun.
Father Bear took Little Bear's paw.
Now they had time to talk.
Just the two of them, father and son, all the way home.